EDIBLE ARRANGMENTS

A NOVELETTE

CASSANDRA B

Edited by
THE EDITING BOUTIQUE

LITERATURE
PUBLICATIONS

ACKNOWLEDGMENTS

Special thank you to Skye - that's my best friend, go best friend.

Think tank for the laughs through this process

Jess - none of this was done without you. Thank you for being you!

Ivy - your encouragement is life.

Ronielle - for being my eight set of eyes when I need it, you are love!

To the reader - thank you for buying, downloading, sharing and supporting this book. This novelette is a little over 19k. If you are looking for a long book by me please explore bit.ly/AUBREEPYNN

ONE

William James

THE SUN HAD NO MERCY.

It was absolutely relentless in beating down on a brother's back. In the past few hours my skin had baked well past done, and the oven's timer was buzzing. It was a burning alarm signaling I needed to get out of this sun before it killed me. Pausing briefly to wipe the sweat pouring down my face with the t-shirt I peeled off an hour into this. "Gah damn. What the hell goin' on out here?"

Every muscle in my body was on fire. I didn't need to work out tonight; I needed to lay in a tub of ice to relax my muscles and baked skin. It was beyond sweltering; felt like the devil was running circles around me.

"I need to go to church. I cannot go to hell. It's hot as hell out here."

It was literally hotter than swamp possum pussy on the fourth of July. This shit didn't make no damn sense.

As I rounded the corner from the side of the house to the front, Mrs. McFee was standing on the porch with a tray of her famous lemonade. I wasn't exaggerating; Mrs. McFee had bottled up some of the best lemonade on this side of the Mississippi and sold it like high-end drugs.

A part of my childhood was teaming up with Weston to sell it on the corner, in town, and for fundraisers we had for whatever sport we called ourselves playing at the time. And there was a lot of shit we tried to do - baseball, basketball, track, and I even think we went and got our asses tackled to impress some girls. Needless to say, the lemonade was crack.

Mrs. McFee literally made lemons into lemonade, and it yielded a very comfortable lifestyle. After Mr. McFee was killed in the War Against Terror, his lady kicked her skills into gear to send both of their children to college. Weston had scholarships but decided to stay back to go to a local college in order to be close to his mother, while Aria darted out of town the first chance she had. Weston wanted to stay and protect his mother, and Aria wanted to go see the world. She was always looking for some sort of adventure.

Removing my AirPods from my ears, I looked up and shot Mrs. McFee a warm smile back. That saved my thoughts from wandering off on Aria - which they did a lot since we were kids. Now that West was gone, she'd been invading my thoughts a lot more than I was comfortable with. And seeing her at the funeral didn't help me rid myself of thoughts of her.

"The yard looks great, Willie. Come take a break," she politely ordered motioning for me to kill the engine on the lawn mower.

While I was walking toward her I was met with a cool breeze, and looked around the yard at the work I'd done so far. Normally, West was here to help me. We would have this done in two hours tops. I missed my boy. Sucking in a sharp breath, I hiked the four stairs of her farmhouse-style home and made myself comfortable on the porch furniture.

"Are you staying for dinner?" she posed the question as though there was an option attached.

I came over every two weeks to fix anything around the house, manicure her lawn, and keep her company for a while. In the beginning, she insisted that she didn't need any help but I knew West would be rolling in his grave if I left his momma hanging. Shit, she was my momma too.

My mother moved shortly after I graduated. She said I was a grown man now and she didn't need to baby me anymore. Where most kids would be ass hurt about it, I took it and strived. I started doing handiwork around town to get me through community college and never stopped. I talked to my mom every week or so, but Mrs. McFee made sure I stayed on the straight and narrow. Even if West wasn't here, I was going to make sure I continued to show her how much I appreciated her.

"I don't know, momma. What did you cook?" I asked jokingly - as I leaned up and rested my elbows on my knees.

She gave a soft knowing look as she set the tray down and took a seat opposite of mine. "Fried chicken, mashed potatoes

3

and gravy, corn on the cob, macaroni and cheese, and peach cobbler."

My mouth watered and my stomach did a dance preparing me for the best meal I had all week. Knowing she would cook like this when I came by, I packed an extra set of clothes to change into. Helping myself to a glass of fresh-squeezed lemonade I shrugged my shoulders. "I don't know, momma. You're trying to make me undesirable to the ladies."

She rolled her eyes without missing a beat and waved me off. "William James, you and I know the truth."

We sure did. It wasn't a secret to her. The first time I came over here and laid eyes on her baby girl - with the wild reddish-brown hair, freckles splashed over her slender nose, bright eyes, and curt smirk - I was in love. First, I thought it was some shit that would fade because we were kids and Aria was meaner than a damn snake. But as we got older, and she grew out and I grew up, I knew she was mine. To this day I regret not making my feelings known. Even if West was going to beat my ass behind it. Maybe she would have stayed home and our lives would have been a lot different.

Maybe not.

"Alright, alright, you don't have to be so loud." I laughed and gulped the contents of the glass so I wouldn't be inclined to say anything that was going to have her summon Aria home and throw her in a room with me. I appreciated her advocating on my behalf and hers, however this was something I needed to handle myself.

Mrs. McFee grew quiet for a minute and looked around the yard at her weeded garden, fresh-cut grass and for a moment I was sure she felt the same thing I felt. "Thank you for doing this, Willie. I know you have your life -"

"I'm going to stop you right there. You know West wouldn't have this any other way, and you already know that my Saturdays are yours."

She smiled coolly and pushed herself up. "Get cleaned up and come eat."

Leaving me on the porch she disappeared into the house. I sat on the porch a few more minutes before I went to retrieve my bag, clean myself up in the guest bathroom, and then joined her at the dining room table.

She always piled my plate high with food, and made multiple to-go containers. I wasn't missing any meals if she had anything to say about it. When she finally joined me, she pushed her hair out of her face and said, "Aria and I went to clean up Weston's house last week. I have some things by the door that he wanted you to have."

I nodded, processing everything she just laid on me. I never knew how he managed to keep his condition a secret from all of us. Initially, I was pissed that I didn't know until the last month - when the cancer had gotten worse and had him bedridden. When I looked back over the last year, he made sure he had his affairs in order without really telling us what was going on.

"Aria's back?" I asked, stopping my thoughts midtrack. How the hell did Aria sneak back into town and I hadn't gotten a whiff of her. "Or did she head back?"

Momma smirked. "She's back for good. Weston left her strict instructions. She's staying in town at those new condos."

"Hmm."

"Hmm," she copied. "I sure hope this time you don't freeze."

"I didn't freeze," I corrected. "I allowed Ladybug to live her life."

Her brows raised and she nodded her head slowly. "Alright, William."

I finished dinner without obsessing over Aria. It was hard as hell. I had to put myself into a position to run into her. She'd already been here a week too long without me seeing her face, inhaling her scent, and wrapping her in an embrace that melted her against me.

"Now, Willie, don't forget that light in the den needs to be changed, too," Mrs. McFee called from the kitchen. She was packing up food and containers of lemonade to get me through the next couple of days.

Lightly chuckling to myself, I shook my head from side to side. I didn't mind because outside of her daughter, I was the closest thing she had to him. Wes didn't have kids or a wife he left behind. It was just us, trying to figure out how we were going to move along without him. He was the glue to all of us, and we missed the hell out of him. Even more, Mrs. McFee missed him tremendously.

I changed the light, scanned the house, and made sure every-thing was good to go before taking the bags of Weston's things to the truck. I walked back up the steps to meet her on the porch.

"This should keep you from having to go to Jenine's and having that nasty ass, thirsty ass, dirty ass Chanel push up on you," she commented with disapproval. I knew what she was up to and I couldn't help but laugh. "I'll see you later, take care of yourself, and call your mother."

"Mrs. McFee." I chuckled and shook my head.

She placed her hands on her hips and looked me up and down. "Did I tell a lie?"

"No ma'am."

"I know I didn't. That girl is damn nasty and you'll be wise not to dive into that polluted back river. You'll pull out with an itch, a burn, and a head full of regret."

"Momma," I grunted while shaking my head.

"Don't *momma* me. You heard what I said?"

"Yes, ma'am," I answered with a laugh.

No woman in Glendale could bat their eyes in my direction without Mrs. McFee getting wind of it and running them off. I had an overnight guest from time to time but as far as relationships went, they were few and far in between. Not because of her, but because of her daughter. No one was Aria, and she knew it.

TWO

A ria McFee

GLENDALE HADN'T CHANGED A BIT. Well, not much outside of the Starbucks that popped up across from Jenine's cafe, and the new condos I was now calling home. When I returned I considered moving back into my momma's. That idea was quickly short-lived when I thought about how intrusive she was. I hadn't been around her pushy personality for years, and I didn't think I could reacclimate myself to her ways at thirty-five years old. Plus, being in town made me feel closer to Weston somehow. The cemetery where we buried him was five minutes away.

Damn, I missed him. It was unreal how much I missed him. It had been windy for the last two days and I swore that West was reminding me that he might have been gone from the body, but his spirit remained ever close to mine. That gave my guilty conscience some ease.

There were days where I hated myself for not coming home sooner. He never told me he wasn't doing well, he just said that I needed to come and see mom, and get away from the city. After my divorce, I should have run back home but my stubbornness and need to prove everyone wrong kept me in Ganton Hills wasting my time.

Now I was charged with a task I had to see all the way through. I couldn't quit halfway in like I was used to. I didn't need Weston popping up in my dreams telling me about myself. Lord knew he did enough of that while he was alive.

I sighed, parked my car, gathered my things, and marched into the town building. I needed to get my permits so that the contractors I already paid could start their work. It never made sense to me that there was barely anyone up here and I still had to take a number, sit in these hard plastic chairs, and wait for one of these lazy sloths to call me to the window. I hated coming here. I hated coming here as much as I hated getting waxed but both were necessary.

I sucked in a sharp breath, took a number and sat down. Crossing my legs, I placed my purse in my lap, pulled my cell phone out, and occupied myself with confirmation notifications from the various vendors who were shipping everything I needed to make Mocha and Merlot the best place in town for gourmet chocolates and wine. Weston wouldn't have it any other way, especially because the two life insurance policies he left for momma and me, wouldn't allow it.

Minutes crept by, and my patience was quickly fleeting. I had a million things to do and being stuck in this bone-chilling brick building was going to drive me absolutely insane. This was the second day of this shit. Yesterday they decided to close after lunch, today I wasn't having it. If I had to jump the

9

counter and stamp these permits myself, I was going to do just that, and see myself out before Sheriff Jones could find me.

"Ticket eighty-four," a raspy unpleasant voice called from behind the counter. I looked around the waiting room, I was the only one here.

With a huff, I pushed myself out of the chair and clacked my pumps over to the counter. I was sure to walk with a bit more authority than normal. When the lady saw my coy smile greet her, her droopy face dropped even more.

"Oh, you're back," she dryly commented.

She was already under my skin thanks to the wait, and not being accepting of people playing in my face.

"Yes, I am. I told you I would be. I have the permits signed, and I'm back for my stamp of approval. If you could be so kind as to stamp them, I'll be out your hair and you'll be on your break. Lord knows you've probably had a tiring day," I shot back in the sweetest voice I could muster up.

She huffed as I slid the permits over with my license. In true old woman fashion, she looked over her glasses at the paperwork and my driver's license. She did this at least twelve times before grunting and sliding them back to me.

"I can't do anything with these."

"Excuse me?" I asked because I was sure I was hearing things. "Come again."

"I cannot do anything with these."

My brows dipped and my pressure rose. "What do you mean you cannot do anything with these?"

My voice copied hers at the end of the comment. Apparently it ticked her off because she was as red as I felt underneath my sepia-toned melanin. "Do you know that I have been jumping through hoops for two days to get these damn things signed and now today there isn't anything you can do about them? You have to be shitting me."

"Your name," she spoke up.

"What about it?" I semi snapped.

"They don't match, Mrs. Evans." The slick grin on her horrid face was asking to be slapped off. Not wanting to be on the sheriff's radar for upholding my reputation and acting up, I straightened the hem of my mustard-colored silk dress and huffed.

Mrs. Evans. A seven-year mistake that was still following me around a year after divorcing his sorry, community dick having ass. Just the thought of the man repulsed me. Coupled with the hag in front of me, I was bound to tear up some shit.

"You see your name on the permit says McFee the name on your license says Ev-"

"Aht!" I held my hand up and shook my head. "Don't you even dare. I will go to the DMV and come back."

"Hm," she huffed. "Not unless you have that divorce decree."

The comment was snide and she was begging for me to put my hands on her, but I swore to my mother I would come back to Glendale refined and changed. I told her I wouldn't fight, curse or assault Sheriff Jones like I was known to do. I sucked in a deep breath and smiled at the hag of a woman.

"Though it isn't any of your damn business, I do. Some of us have enough sense to leave the tired old man," I mildly returned, taking my things. "Like I said before you suggested I slapped you in the mouth, I will be back."

"Hmph, not today we closed three minutes ago."

"I swear to God, I hate this town."

"Then you should probably go back to Ganton Hills with the rest of the city folk without home training."

Before I slapped the dentures out of her mouth I graciously gave her a warning glare and turned to walk away. Strutting out of the town building across the street in my six-inch heels, I walked into the DMV and waited impatiently for my number to be called. Thank God they seemed a little more efficient than the billy goat I just dealt with.

Walking out of the DMV with an official name change and an attitude, I reached my car and decided to go see my mother. I hadn't seen her since we finished cleaning out Weston's house last week. The realtor was coming to do the final walk-through in a week, and momma and I had worked tirelessly making sure everything was good to go.

It took me thirty minutes to get to her house. The second I pulled up, the irritation fell from my shoulders. Parking my car behind hers, I stepped out and looked around the yard. It was beautiful. The flower bed had been weeded out, the grass was cut, and the lights leading up the porch had been replaced.

"Ma," I called walking into the house and peeling my heels off my tired feet. "Who did the yard?"

I walked straight to the fridge knowing she had something leftover in there for me to eat. Dad had been gone for years, and Weston had been gone for almost three months now so I needed to know who she called herself cooking for. I was praying it wasn't Mr. Floyd up the street. He'd been sniffing around for a while, and momma was never clear on whether she was baking his pies or giving him the pie.

Finding some leftover spaghetti, I fixed myself a plate and roamed into the living room where she was avidly watching the five o'clock news. She glanced up and did a once over. "You look nice."

"Thanks, I had business to handle but everyone in this damn town is slow and rude as hell," I muttered with a mouth full of food.

Mom laughed softly and looked at me again. "Aria you are the one who is mean as hell. And that's my fault I couldn't stand anyone when I was carrying you. Not even your daddy,that's why you look just like him with softer features."

"Did you just say that I looked like a gentleman?" I asked, cracking a smile.

"I did, and you did." We shared a laugh and she decided to hit me with the gut punch. "Willie James came by and did the yard for me on Saturday. I told him you were back so please don't run from him."

I'd been ducking William James Bernett for the last month and hadn't run into him or spotted the rusty orange pick up truck. Willie James would make me forget my damn religion and never turn back. When I saw him at the funeral I lost my words. He grew up. He wasn't that lanky boy bothering me every three seconds. He was fine. I mean wide back, country fed, rough around the edges, big hands, and feet to match, had every woman in town swooning after him fine. He was not to be trifled with, and I wasn't going to let him trifle with me.

"Ma you need to let that little dream go. That isn't the Lord's will."

"And Aria McFee how would you know? You haven't seen the Lord and He hasn't heard your cry in years. Because Lord knows had He heard it you wouldn't have married that dreadful man."

"Momma, I heard it from you and Weston several times. I don't want to hear it again. Let it ride, lady."

"Aria, I'll let it ride when you start riding."

I damn near choked. "You are awful."

"And you know you want that man. Shit, if I could get my leg up high enough I would have him. Show him a few things or twenty"

"You are nasty."

"And you got it from your momma. Act like you know what's good. Say hi to the man when you see him."

THREE

W illiam

"HEY, WILLIE!"

I didn't even look over my shoulder when I heard the voice, I knew exactly who it was. Every day I had to come into town to pick up something was another day where Chanel needed to bring her ass out of the cafe and holler at me. I threw a nod in her direction and finished loading the bed of my truck up with lumber, paint, and a few other miscellaneous things.

I rounded the back of the tailgate to climb into the driver's seat before Chanel could make her way over here and ask me to fix something. The last time I did that, she popped up in the kitchen in little to nothing and cornered me. After I escaped my big ass through her window I vowed to never do that shit again.

Mrs. McFee's warning rang loud in my head and I sure as hell wasn't about to tell her that I got myself into some shit. If you let Chanel tell it I was sweet on her and that was the furthest thing from the truth.

Just as I cranked up my pick up, I spotted *her*. The beautiful face that had been haunting me since I was fifteen. As fast as I turned the engine on, I turned it off and scrambled out the truck like a lovestruck teenage boy.

"Willie, I got some pipes that need to be cleaned," Chanel called as I started across the parking lot to Aria. Her and those damn pipes could go to hell.

"Aria!"

Aria looked over her shoulder at me, and my heart damn near stopped. She saw me and kept walking. She could have easily irritated me with her stubbornness but that's not how I wanted our meeting to go today. I chuckled softly to myself and casually followed her into the storefront.

When I walked in I inhaled the dust that was flying around the abandoned storefront. I propped the door open and looked around. "You bought Gerald's?"

Aria looked good enough to eat. I could start at her lips and finish at her toes. She stood in the middle of the old creamery that posed as the after game hang-out in high school. After Gerald died, his family moved to Brighton Heights and left his shop behind for the town to close down.

I scanned my eyes over the area and back to Aria who was in deep thought. Either that or she was trying to wish me away. Either way, it was fine by me for the time being. It gave me time to take in her sweet floral scent along with how damn

16

good she looked in those jeans that hugged every curve. The high heel sandals she wore only lifted her round ass up more. As my eyes trailed up they landed on her gracious set of breasts.

"Did you follow me in here to stare at me?" she asked, dropping her arms from across her full chest to her hips.

I gleamed softly at her as she squinted up at me with that curl of her lip that always made me want to lean down and nibble it away. Aria was still as beautiful as ever. Even more gorgeous than my memory served. "No, I came over to say hello since you ducking and dodging me like the plague."

She huffed and shook her head in laughter. "Hello, Willie. How are you?"

Aria couldn't even keep her eyes on me long enough for me to adore her ember orbs.

"Now that I've seen you Ladybug, I'm good," I commented watching her walk away to her purse. "So you're back and opening up shop?"

"Weston left strict instructions in his will and I don't play around with the dead," she answered with her back still turned to me.

Again, I had a moment to adore her. If she only knew how bad I wanted to snatch her pretty ass up and take her right here. She wasn't ready for that, she was still standoffish and in her head. Although she was beautiful and put together on the outside I felt the heaviness she was carrying. We carried the same sadness. Weston was our brother; hers by blood, mine by choice. I wanted to ask her how she was really doing but her attitude was already brewing and I didn't want to get my head bitten off.

"You know if you need any help, I got you," I spoke up again.

This time she turned around to study me. Her eyes traveled me from the top of my head down to my feet, a curt smirk crossed her face, and a small fire sparked in her eyes. That tiny flame was felt between us. It had always been. However, both of us never blew on it to make it grow. I wanted to take a step forward but she took a step back.

"I have some contractors that are on their way, but thank you," she politely answered. That was my cue to get the hell out of dodge before she had to forcibly tell my black ass to get out of here. Although, if she got feisty, I could snatch her up.

I licked my lips, flashed her a kind smile, and said, "I'll be seeing you around, Ladybug. But if you need me, I'm a call away. Weston would haunt my ass if I let you come home and struggle with anything."

She chuckled and flashed me another look. "Weston didn't play about any of us.I know if he were here, he'd get in my ass about being stubborn, but rest assured, I got it. Plus, Miss Glendale is looking for your attention."

I dropped my head back and groaned in full blown irritation. Outside of being ignored and counted out, Chanel irritated me more than any of that. "That damn woman."

"Ah, don't do that. I know you, Willie James. You're a ladies man." Aria laughed and waved her tiny finger at me. Her smile was bright enough to light up the deepest depths of my soul. It was the brightest beam of golden sunray to hit this earth.

I frowned. She didn't know the half about what kind of man I was exactly, and she was pussyfooting around delaying the process to find out for herself. I started off to open the door just as casually as I walked in. I needed my presence to linger, Aria needed my aura to invade hers even after I was gone. "I'm a one-woman man, Ladybug. You'll see. Be sure to leave this door open while you're in here."

"I'll do that," she replied softly watching me walk away. "Take care of yourself."

"You do the same, Ladybug."

FOUR

ria

LADYBUG.

I had a love-hate relationship with the name. A simple term of endearment had become so much more to me. If Willie were to call me anything else besides that, it would sound foreign to me. On the other hand it would have irritated me deeply that he called me anything but.

Thanks to me being deathly terrified of bugs, Ladybug had stuck with my grown ass since childhood. When the word slid through his full rosewood lips it was the most beautiful thing I had ever heard. Willie James was going to press me like this was a full-court action, and once he got started he didn't stop. Not that I wasn't immune to it by now. I knew how he moved and what he came with, but could he really be as sweet and as warm as I felt right now?

I hated it when momma was right. I also hated that I had to fight so hard to keep myself from melting every time Willie James was around. In the beginning, he was just as annoying as Weston. Also, Weston's friends were not supposed to be on my radar - but Willie. Willie managed to always swindle his way into my mind and leave his impression on me. And like a school girl giggling after the mention of the popular jock, I was useless until the feeling faded.

Tugging on the corner of my lip until his beat-up orange pick-up truck disappeared down the street, I released a faint sigh of relief. I was happy he was gone but I wanted him to turn back around and invade my space again.

"Aria, will you pull yourself together?" I fussed silently at myself.

Moving on from my wayward thoughts about Willie and his thick caramel, tattooed, tall, cornbread fed, defensive end built, body of an African god. Shit, the thought alone had me wanting to take off down the street in these heels so I could climb him like a tree.

Rallying my attention fully, I scanned the parking lot between my storefront and Jenine's for the contractors. They were supposed to be here by now. Daylight was wasting away. By the time they got here it would be time to call it a day and try again in the morning. It had already taken me almost a week to get the permits I needed to start. This shop was posing to be a lot more difficult than I thought it would be.

After almost forty-five minutes of calling, attempting to sweep the building up myself I threw the towel in. I was choking off of the dust and I knew better to be in here alone after the sun went down. Collecting my things and securing the door, I headed down the sidewalk only to be met by the voice of the town tramp.

"I see you and Willie are sweet on each other again," Chanel's tone was laced with jealousy and assumptions.

"You know what they say," I started with a coy smile as I hit the button on my key fob to start my car. "When you assume you make an ass out of yourself. Enjoy your night."

I was too tired to get into a pissing match about who he belonged or didn't belong to. I didn't have a stake in him, just lude thoughts. Willie was fine and familiar. I was horny and neglected. It was a dangerous mix.

I got in my car and pulled off. I was so aggravated I didn't even stop by my apartment. I went straight to mommas. Pulling my duffle bag off the back seat, I stomped into the house and kicked my heels off my feet.

"Why do you look like you and a dust mop got into a fight?" she asked, meeting me at the door.

"Because a dust mop and I did get into a fight," I huffed shuffling down to the guest bathroom.

Peeling the layers of dusty clothes off of my body, I hopped in the shower and then joined momma on the couch.

"You insisted on getting your own spot and yet you're here," she muttered looking at me cozy up on the other end of the couch in my silk pajamas.

"I mean, I can leave since you're going to act like I'm cock blocking."

"You are cock blocking," she announced.

"Momma!"

"Aria!"

"Who and why?"

"Willie, because you don't appreciate a fine piece of ass when you see it," she replied with a snicker.

I huffed and rolled my eyes. "I am not doing this with you tonight."

"You should be doing him tonight. You would be in a much better mood. Speaking of which, why are you in such a mood?" she quizzed.

"The contractors I paid never showed up and didn't answer any of my calls. I am livid and out of two thousand dollars. Not to mention, I ran around this slow ass town for days for a new license and a stamp. A stamp. I just want to sleep."

"You need some dick," she started up again.

"Momma!" I groaned. "Please stop it."

"Okay, okay," she conceded, throwing her hands up. "On a serious note, I don't know why you didn't ask Willie. He does good work, and he's efficient."

I gritted my teeth and shot her a look out the corner of my eye. She had no idea what that man's presence did to me and if she knew, she would have been a lot more persistent about it than she was. "I am not asking William James for anything."

"But you should. You're just being stubborn, and it is very unbecoming of you. The man will drop everything for you. Everyone knows that. Hell, Weston knew that."

23

"Weston isn't here to attest that."

"I tell you no lies. The man is sweet on you like the chocolate you sell and has been since he waltzed his scrawny ass into this house. Call him in the morning and get your shop together."

I pushed myself out of the deep cushions and started off down the hall. "Goodnight, momma."

"Dream of Willie."

"I should have taken my ass home."

When I got into my old room everything instantly became heavier. I teetered on the edge of the bed and looked around at the things my mother left intact. After dad died, she left everything the same - the paint, the fixtures, and anything else that he touched. You could feel him all in the strokes. It was the same with Weston. The need to still feel both of them was overwhelming, and probably why I found myself here more than at the place I was paying to live in.

Major pieces of my life were taken from me, and I wasn't sure how I was still surviving. I supposed I got it from her. It was an unspoken perseverance that was a part of my genetic makeup. I was Deloris and Frank's daughter. I had fight, determination, and the ability to bounce back, but this was far more than I fantomed.

Feeling her at the door, I invited her in but didn't move my eyes from the spot on the wall. My tears hadn't fallen over West yet, or my failed marriage. It felt like I'd been holding my breath, waiting to exhale with the security of knowing that nothing else was going to throw my world off-kilter again.

Momma sat by me and wrapped her arms around my shoulders. "Breathe. Accept it all as it is, and allow God to fill the voids. Whatever is on the way for you is far greater than what you imagined."

FIVE

illiam

I WAS BURIED under corroded pipes, rusty water, and an overbearing client. I never understood why people hired me to do something for them only to stand over me and either attempt to help, or tell me how to do the damn job. At this point I was willing to run into town for something I didn't need just to get away from Mr. Simon and his unwarranted help.

"Willie, all you got to do is bang them there pipes on out with the wrench and duct tape that hole up, it'll be fine," he shared hanging over the sink looking down at me.

Everything he said was mushed due to him not wanting to put his teeth in his mouth unless he was going into town. Thank God the sink was collecting the spit flying. It was already bad enough that I was drenched in dirty water. Mr. Simon was at least eighty-two and banging pipes out with wrenches and patching them with duct tape was how we got in this situation in the first place.

"Well, Mr. Simon. your pipes are no good so I have to replace everything," I responded coming from underneath the sink to grab the new pipe. "I'll have everything brand new in just a minute."

He winced slightly. "Boy that's gon cost more money than a whore from main street!"

I couldn't help but laugh as I pried the old pipe off. It was shit like this that kept me in Glendale, pure comedy. "Mr. Simon, don't worry about it. I got it."

I could feel his slack smile cross his face. "Boy, no wonder you still livin' here, you ain't making no money."

The man didn't hold shit back. Hell, when I got up there I wanted to be the same way. At this point what was he holding his tongue for. "Mr. Simon, you don't have nothing else to do?"

"Nah," he answered. "I leave you alone for two minutes and then the wife comes waltzing in here trying to put something on you. I'm trying to save your life boy. 'Cause you start grinning too hard at her I'm gon have to shank ya big ass."

I shook my head and focused back on the task at hand. My stomach was growling and I wanted to get out of here before I had to deal with Mrs. Simon. Out of all the women in the town, she had the strength to take advantage of me and I wasn't trying to go out like that. How these old women were so strong was beyond me. I wasn't no little boy either.

Finishing up the job, I collected my supplies and jogged down the porch to throw everything into the bed of my truck. I had a few hours between my next job. I was going to head home, wash this shit off of me and tackle the rest of those left overs from Mrs. McFee.

Before I could pull the truck out the driveway, my phone rang. I glanced down at the unsaved number and frowned a bit. Swiping the icon, I pressed the phone to my ear. "Willie James."

"Willie, hi." Her sweet voice hit my ears and immediately I perked up.

I relaxed some and settled into the seat. "Aria, what do I owe the pleasure?"

Her tone was a lot softer than normal which meant she needed something. I was prepared to see how far around the bush she was going to beat before asking me for help.

"Nothing," she replied slowly. "I just - um - just wanted to call and say hi. That's all."

I laughed and palmed the top of my head. "Just to say hi, huh? You sure that's all?

"Mhmm, that's all. I'll talk to you later," she quipped, trying to get out of whatever she'd gotten herself into.

"No you won't. Tell me what you need. I won't let you hang up without telling me," I gently pushed.

I imagined her tugging at her lip while she toyed with asking me for help or attempting to do whatever by herself.

"I don't need any-"

"I know you, Ladybug. Tell me how I can be of service to you."

She took a deep breath and exhaled. "My contractors pulled out on me at the last minute with my damn money but that's neither here nor there. Do you have any openings in your demanding schedule to help me with this mess?"

"Are you at the shop now?"

"I am."

"I'll be there in about thirty minutes," I shared. "And Lady-bug, whatever you're doing please stop."

"I wasn't doing nothing," she defended in a pitchy voice. I could see her hide whatever she was holding behind her back and beaming those beautiful eyes up at me sheepishly, in my head.

"Uh huh, I'll see about that."

"Thank you, Willie."

"Don't even mention it."

Ending our call, I searched my truck for another shirt, I always kept a clean one on hand incase of emergencies. I changed my shirt, pulled out the driveway and settled with the idea of grabbing a sandwich from the cafe when I got into town.

The thirty-minute drive was cut down to twenty. When Aria called, which she rarely did, I didn't waste any time getting to her. I wasn't going to give her time to rethink her decision and back out on me. I had her in my grasp and if I had to save the day to get her closer to me, that's what I was willing to do.

The second I walked into the shop I couldn't help but laugh. Aria had traded in her high heels, expensive fabrics, and her pressed hair for a baseball cap, oversized t-shirt, leggings, and sneakers. The sneakers looked like this was the first day they saw sunlight. On top of all that she was covered in paint from the top of her head down to her brand new sneakers.

"Don't laugh at me Willie," she whined. "I tried to do it on my own."

"And we see how that turned out," I said ceasing my laughter to look around then back at her. "Why are you painting?"

She shrugged. "I honestly don't have a clue of what I'm doing. I just wanted to do something."

"Well, I appreciate your need to be productive but this place needs a lot more than some paint and a beautiful owner. You have electricity issues, the plumbing is probably bad and you have a bug problem," I pointed out seeing a few spiders scurry across the floor.

Aria screeched and jumped into my arms. Laughing again, I held on to her and sat her on the counter. "Still haven't gotten over that, huh?"

Aria lightly punched my chest. "It's your fault! You and those damn spiders. I will never be the same."

I may or may not have dropped a spider in her hair when we were kids. "I can't help that I was a kid and couldn't express my puppy love."

She nudged me away, rolled her eyes and changed the subject. "How much is all this going to run me?"

"What are you doing with this place anyway?" I asked bypassing her question. Aria knew her money was no good here. I wanted her heart, and everything else in between.

"Really, you're just going to ignore my question like that?" she sassed.

I turned to her, swiped the smudge of paint from her cheek and watched how her sepia skin deepened. With a smirk and a lick of the lips, I spoke up again, "What are you doing with this place?"

"Mocha and Merlot. A wine bar and chocolate shop," she replied with a beam. "It's been my dream forever, life just changed currents on me for a while."

"Well, there's no better time than now. What's your timeframe?"

"I have supplies showing up in a few weeks. Can you please tell me how much it's going to cost to get everything fixed?"

"Ladybug your money's no good here," I replied while I started walking around to get a better look at what this place really needed. That, and I was trying to keep my hands off of her.

"Hmm," she buzzed. "No wonder you're still a hometown boy."

I halted in mid stride as my brows dipped in. "What does that mean, Aria?"

She looked at me oddly after hearing her given name and not what she was used to. I felt like she tried me lowkey, and I needed to know what she meant before I put her back in her place.

"You can't just turn down money for services you do, Willie," she replied. "I mean if you actually charged what you were worth you wouldn't have to drive that beat up truck everyday. When was the last time you dressed up? The last time you wore a suit was when? Prom and West's funeral?"

Yeah, my baby was trying the hell out of me.

I made my way back over to her to look in her face before I made my way out of here. "You haven't been home in years. Your perception of everything is skewed. I could go anywhere in the world that I want, Aria. I chose to stay here because this is my home and I love it. And I don't have a need to wear a suit every day. What I do doesn't require one. I work with my hands. Everything that I have comes from these two hands. Would you like to find out?"

I watched her eyes study mine and then drop in embarrassment. "I'll email you the invoice."

She had no words; she just started gnawing on that lip. I wanted to snatch her ass up and take over the work to her lip, but she needed to sit with that shit for a day or two. I'm not sure what kind of men she was used to dealing with in the city, but it wasn't me. She wasn't going to discredit my hard work because of what she saw.

"Have a good day, Ms. McFee." I walked out and climbed into my truck. If she wanted business, she had it until I felt like she deserved more.

SIX

ria

"HAVE A GOOD DAY, MS. MCFEE."

Everytime I thought about those six words my lips curled and my stomach turned. Willie rarely called me Aria let alone Ms. McFee. The last time I heard that was shortly after I got married and he refused to call out my married name. I mean downright refused. He would have rather died than call me Mrs. Evans.

For six hours I couldn't get the look in his eyes out my head. I felt like I disrespected him in the worst way. Willie was a proud man. The pick up truck was all he had left of his dad, and I could easily admit that he worked his ass off. The people in this town loved the hell out of him. Some may have liked him a little too much for my liking, but nevertheless they did. It had always been that way.

Willie wasn't the type to run with the wrong crowd or pretend to be anything that he wasn't. He was just Willie. Easy to love, trust, and rely on. How he wasn't snatched up by now was beyond me. Hell, if I had a clue back then, I would have done it myself.

I didn't like this feeling. I needed to make it right before tomorrow. Not only did I need my shop together, I needed him not to be mad at me. I couldn't handle that too long. Now that I thought about it, who knew how long he'd really been upset with me, and my decision to leave and never look back. Willie did everything but beg me to stay or tell me how he really felt.

Most of it was out of respect for Weston. Lord forbid Willie and I acted on impulses and we didn't work out, leaving West in the middle to choose.

I sucked in a deep breath. "West, I don't know what you're doing. But I don't like it."

Shuffling into my kitchen to pour the remainder of the bottle of wine into my glass, I hoisted myself on the counter. I let my legs swing while I went back and forth with myself on whether or not to be stubborn. I could apologize now or stall this out. But it would only make everything awkward.

As I scrolled through my emails, I saw his invoice. Opening the attachment I wasn't surprised that it was far less than he should really be charging me. In the email was a request to schedule the next three weeks out so he could ensure his availability.

"Okay, Willie," I huffed, closing out the emails and hitting his number. "I'll give you what you want."

The line rang a few times before he answered. "You're calling me after hours. I'm going to have to charge you, Ms. McFee."

"Well add it to my invoice, we should probably schedule the next three weeks," I responded with an eye roll.

"Not without an apology."

"Huh?"

"Oh Ladybug, you are neither deaf nor dumb. Listen, I know you've been away dealing with that sucka ass nigga that didn't know how to be a man. And that's cool if that's how you like them, but I ain't that type. I give you the utmost respect because you deserve that shit. I require the same. Now, you need work done, and I need an apology."

I was stuck for a second. I think he put me in my place so gently I didn't notice I was there until I was there. I looked around the kitchen like he was standing in front of me with those demanding warm eyes. I would do virtually anything just for them to grace my flesh. Shit, when he held me earlier I wanted to stay there but I knew that going down this road with Willie could either be so amazing or terribly tumultuous.

With a deep breath, I said in the softest way I could conjure up, "I'm sorry, Willie. I will never disrespect you again. Can we please schedule the next few weeks?"

"No," he cooly replied.

I could just see him over there laid back with that unbothered expression on his face. It was the smirk that could soak the seat of my panties and urge me to smother him as a result.

"No?" I repeated like a parakeet. "I just apologized to you."

"That isn't the apology I need, Aria."

I raised my brow and pulled my phone away from my ear. Against my better judgement, I hit the facetime icon so I could see his face. He wasted no time switching over. Just like I thought that damn smirk was on full display over those beautiful pair of lips.

"You needed to see my face to understand what I was telling you?" he asked.

"Yes, because I apologized."

He lightly laughed, scratched his chin through his beard. "No you didn't, Ladybug."

I clenched my thighs and took a deep breath. "Okay, what do you want Willie?"

"Dinner."

"Dinner?" I asked quickly, drawing my neck back.

He laughed again. "You heard me, and you read my lips. I saw you."

I rolled my eyes. "I'm going to hang up on you."

"You called me. These are my demands. Agree to dinner and we can get this schedule going."

I chewed on the inside of my cheek while we stared at each other for a moment. "Would you like me to give you a reason to chew on your cheek?"

Yes, just like I want to see what your hands can do.

I gulped snapping myself out of it. "Okay, when and where?"

"Tomorrow at my house, around seven."

I knew that if I weren't careful I was going to be undressed on his lap dripping this honey all over him. I was going to go, but I was going to wear the biggest panties I owned. Taking a deep breath I nodded.

"I need to hear you agree. A, *"yes, Willie"* will work."

Rolling my eyes and curling my lip like saying it was going to kill me. "Yes, Willie. Do I need to bring anything?"

"Just your beautiful self." He was so damn smooth. Why was I being tortured like this? It was an aching at the meeting of my thighs that I was going to have to handle myself just so I could function tomorrow and not want to jump his bones.

Shaking the thought from my head, I returned back to the conversation.

"Who's cooking?"

"Don't worry about the details. I got this. Go get some rest, Ladybug."

"Goodnight, Willie."

I hung up, slid off the counter and grabbed my glass of wine. I was going to attempt to sleep off this feeling. The more my thighs rubbed against each other and applied pressure to my aching center, I knew I had a job to do in order for peaceful sleep. I went straight to my bedroom to retrieve my black and gold sona wave massager.

Truly the best thing created for a single woman although, I was putting it to good use when I was married. It was better than any man I had. It was an amazing orgasm without a headache. I didn't need to set the mood, I just needed to get rid of this ache. With my legs sprawled out on my bed, I shut my eyes, positioned it perfectly over my clit, and set it to my favorite speed and vibration. A complication of gradual speeds to pull this ache out, and allow me to sleep without seeing his face.

With my eyes clenched close and my back arched, all I could see was Willie hovered over me, gracing my skin with his lips while he filled me up. He was close and filling my nostrils with his scent while interlocking my fingers in his. The vibrations were causing my toes to curl while my mind was visualizing Willie's body gliding over mine with ease. Five minutes later I was moaning loudly through my apartment.

After catching my breath, I hissed. "That didn't do shit but make me want dick even more."

I glanced at the time and groaned. "Me, myself, and round two."

Another two rounds and a cold shower, I was finally ready to sleep. This was pathetic.

SEVEN

illie

I BARELY SLEPT LAST NIGHT. My body was doing some wild shit in response to seeing Ladybug on my screen with her titties on display. She did this thing to me and I never recovered. Time after time, and I was tired of it. We were grown and from the way I read the situation it was mutual. She wasn't going to make the first move. She was going to hide behind the veil of respect for Weston. But she didn't even know half of it.

Downing the energy drink and putting the bottle back in the cup holder, I pulled my body out of my truck and headed inside of the grocery store. I know she was probably expecting some take out for dinner. I was going to do her one better. I had close to eight hours to whip up a meal that was going to knock her socks off.

Tonight wasn't about making her mine. I had to put my best foot forward and pick her brain. I had to take into consideration that she'd been through the wringer once and needed assurance that it wasn't going to happen again. Tonight was solely dedicated to planting seeds.

I pushed the buggy down the aisles collecting the things my mother texted me earlier. I refused to tell her that Aria was back until I knew I had it in the bag. Double-checking my list I had a few things left to grab and dart out of here before someone saw me, and needed me to fix something.

I swore staying here was a blessing and a curse. I loved being around and helping, I also loved my time to myself. Which was why I never left my house unless I had to. A brother needed a minute to regroup.

Turning the corner to the check out line after grabbing the last of my list, that cringy ass voice hit my ears. My shoulders hiked up, my head dropped, and I wanted to disappear. "Willie James Bernett."

Sucking in a sharp breath, I briefly looked over my shoulder at Chanel. At first, I was trying to figure out what the hell she had on. It was some type of onesie that wrapped around, buckled, and tied. It looked like it was dipped in glitter and ran through a kaleidoscope, and somehow she squeezed into it. It was the brightest thing I'd ever seen anyone wear in the daylight.

My lip curled, and I couldn't even control that shit. I was dripping in disgust. For the sake of being polite - like I was raised to be - I wearily replied.

"Chanel George."

"I've been trying to get your attention all week. But I see Mrs. Evans has beat me to it," the jealousy dripping from her voice turned my stomach. That, and this glitter contraption she decided to wear out of the house.

"Ms. McFee," I corrected.

"What?" she asked with some stank.

"Ms. McFee," I repeated.

"Wasn't she married to some big time banker? Where is he?"

I shrugged. "Probably in hell. I'm sorry, Chanel was there something you needed or..."

"Well, I just wanted to say hi. And whenever Miss McFee releases you, I have some more plumbing for you to look at," she said with a bat of the eyes.

My stomach turned again. I was about to throw up. Refusing to answer her, I walked off to the check-out line praying this young girl behind the counter hurried up and got me out of here. Once I cleared the grocery store, I went home and got ready for this evening. My nerves were high. I needed to play this as cool as possible.

The doorbell rang jolting me into action. The house was clean, the wine was chilling, dinner was ready. Everything was ready for Aria to walk in and light this place up with her energy. I double checked the details before strolling to the door and cooly opening it for her.

A soft smile crossed her glossed lips as she looked up at me. "You look nice."

"Yeah, I had to make sure you ate those words from yesterday," I teased, making her roll her eyes and attempt to turn around on her heels.

Swiftly catching her by the wrist, I pulled her inside. "Don't even start with your little attitude."

"Little attitude?" she raised her brow and looked me up and down. "I don't know what you're talking about."

"Oh, yeah?"

She smirked. "No idea."

Ladybug spun around and froze. "Wow."

She took in the open floor plan of what used to be my mother's small house. Everything was gutted out and new. Granite and stainless steel in the kitchen, recessed lighting throughout the house, hardwood floors, burnt orange sofa, and the rustic touch made my old child home a warm house to unwind in.

I stood back and crossed my arms over my chest. "You like it?"

"It's beautiful, who designed all of this? Did your mom come back from Lavendale to do this?" she asked, pulling her heels off of her feet and walking deeper into the house.

Studying her as she touched the leather sofa and fixtures, my heart swelled. I could stay in this moment forever with her. "No, I did it myself. I had to occupy myself with something when you left me here with a broken heart."

Aria darted me a look over her shoulder and rolled her eyes. "Stop it, you have every woman in town trying to make an honest man out of you."

"And none of them is the one I want."

When she turned around I was standing there relishing the lust that danced in her eyes as they trailed my body before reaching my eyes. They connected, holding a gaze that was begging for me to take her and put my name on it. She lightly nibbled on her lip before clearing her throat.

"You need something to drink?"

"Wine, please."

I nodded and led her to the dining room where the signature wine from her line was resting in the marble wine chiller. When she took notice to it, a soft smirk crossed her lips and she flashed me a soft look over her shoulder. "Who put you on to this?"

"I've been on. You thought I was going to let you go be great and not invest in your success? I got a few cases downstairs in the basement, too."

"William," she crooned, taking a seat. "You are full of surprises."

"Anything to keep that smile on your face."

She smiled harder and brighter. "Stop it."

"Nah, I like this too much," I commented, wandering off into the kitchen to fix our plates.

After I returned with them and we blessed the food, she took her signature deep breath and glanced across the table at me. "Willie, I'm really sorry about my comment. You have definitely shut me up."

"And we know how hard it is to shut you up."

"Hmm," she started like she had something else she wanted to say. "When Weston told me you remodeled your old house I wasn't expecting this."

She was changing the subject, that was fine. I was riding this wave to wherever she wanted to go. But only for so long before I took control of the boat.

"I was trying to talk him into buying his own and starting up a business with me. I didn't know he was sick, though," I mentioned stopping briefly. "I'm sorry, I don't want this to get heavy."

"I'm not going to stop you. You spent a hell of a lot more time with him than I did. Especially toward the end. He always talked about how good you were doing, though. He tried to make me come back so many times."

"Why didn't you?" I studied the way her shoulders slumped as she buried her hand in her hair.

"I don't know. Embarrassment, shame and not wanting to come back here a failure," she shared. "You know, all the shit that comes along with marrying the wrong man."

I scoffed lightly. "The right man has been in your face for years."

Something clicked inside of me. I was tired of hearing about that fraction of a man she tied herself to. Standing up from my seat, I moved closer to her and took her hand in mine. Weston would pop me upside my head for pussyfooting around with this. If I learned anything from his passing, it was that time wasn't on our side and I needed to put this shit on the table today.

"Waiting on you to just look back. What's blocking you from me, Ladybug?"

She took her bottom lip between her teeth and the jolt of lust flashed in her eyes again. It took her a moment to pull herself out of it and huffed. "Willie…"

Aria reluctantly pulled her hand from my custody and tucked her lip between her teeth. She wanted to give into me, I felt it all in her pulse. The shock that caused her to pull slightly. "This is just dinner, remember? An apology. I didn't come over here for you to smooth talk me and sex me crazy."

Her body was saying everything but. By the way she walked I knew she hadn't experienced good loving in years. The sway in her hips could be loosened if she were bent over at the right angle.

I chuckled, lightly ridding my head of the nasty ass thoughts of her running through my mind. Standing up, I licked my lips before placing a delicate kiss to her forehead. "Ladybug, rest assured this is just dinner. When you grant me permission, I'll explore your temple. Intently, leaving nothing neglected. Understand?"

She shuddered as she nodded, eyes darting signals that she wasn't ready for me to answer.

"Good, eat up. Dinner is getting cold."

EIGHT

ria

I WAS STANDING in a field surrounded by sunflowers of planted seeds from my meddling mother and persistent ass Willie. It was beautiful, vivid, and fragrant. So much so, I wanted to run away and hide. This shit was just as suffocating as it was warm to the taste, and sweet to the touch. I was living in a never ending loop of soft caresses to the cheek, endearing kisses to the forehead, long glances that lingered, and tender brushes across the knuckles.

William James Bernett was trying to drive my ass absolutely insane. Convinced that he was trying to have me broken and bent to his will, I tried to stay clear of him. I couldn't, though. Everywhere I was, Willie would pop up. Whether it was checking on the electricians, plumbers, painters or to ogle at me, Willie made sure I saw him everyday.

After almost an hour of becoming one with my black and gold massager, I finally was out of my house. I used it so much this week that I had to charge it twice. It was resting on my nightstand getting some juice for the pressure I needed to release when I got home because I knew Willie was going to do something to get a rise out of me.

I was stalling. From the time I left my house until now, I was finding everything else to do but go to the shop and see him, and smell him, and want to kick everyone out so I could sit this ass in his lap and stop playing these games.

After meaningless driving in circles I ended up at the cemetery. I hadn't been here since we said our final goodbyes and Willie pulled me into the warmest, securest embrace I'd had in a long time. My ex-husband didn't even hug me like that. Everything with him was quick and cold.

"I can't even go stare at the headstone without thinking about that man," I huffed as I sauntered off down the paved path to the row where we laid Weston's body to rest. "And only one of them should be buried here."

I smelled the air and was violated by the smell of fresh cut grass and dirt. Groaning in annoyance of how my sinuses were going to flare up, I stopped short of West's headstone. This was easier than I thought it would be. I was expecting this to be a fit of tears and snot but I felt ok, finally accepting the fact that Weston was at peace.

"Hey West." I placed my hand on the head tomb and faintly smiled. "I know you're not in there. Just a very costly piece of marble we put next to daddy to give momma some peace that you were in good company. You think you're slick. I be

47

feeling you around. I know that you're pushing Willie and I together, and I have to admit I don't like it."

I laughed and swiped a lone tear from my cheek. "I don't like it because I want you here to see this. But I suppose you're watching from the clouds or the tree over there. Maybe I should stop making excuses and just dive in head first and see where this takes me, right? Like one of my old adventures. Okay...I just figured this out."

I glanced over to dad's headstone and smiled brighter. "You two take care of each other up there okay? I got momma."

Sucking up the rest of my emotion and blowing a double kiss to the head stones, I released an inaudible sigh. The walk back to the car was just as slow as it was before I stopped at the headstones to talk to the wind. I had to suck it up and face the music. Inventory was showing up from my chocolatiers, and there were probably twenty cases of wine that needed to be unpacked and put up.

I walked into the shop and smirked around at the progress. Weston would love this. I had to laugh as I moved further into the building. My brother bullied me into pursuing my dream full time by leaving me. It was hilarious and morbid at the same time. He knew that I would have never done this without the push. I would have stayed in Ganton Hills trying to piece my life back together.

Pushing my curls out of my face and straightening the sheer sleeves on my blouse as I pranced by Willie. He was perched on the ladder fixing a light. I kept my eyes on the stockroom. As hard as it was for me to not look back at him work or ogle over me, I stuck to my course. It was easy to get caught up in him. All of him. If I turned around to say hello I would be drooling and daydreaming over his wide shoulders. The thought of digging my fresh manicure into them caused heat to flood my veins.

I forced a sigh through my lips to reset myself and to dive into work. It took me an hour or so to get all the chocolate unpacked and stored correctly. Moving on to the cases of wine, I glanced over my shoulder to see Willie hard at work.

"Alright, Aria," I muttered to myself as I put the last of the wine bottles away.

The rest of the crew had already breaked for lunch and Willie was still working. Straightening my blouse again, I walked out and carefully leaned on a dry wall. "Have you eaten?"

Willie paused what he was doing to look at me and then resumed his work.

Curling my lip in response, my feet led me in front of the ladder. I looked up at him. "Do you want to go to Jenine's?"

"Oh, you see me?" he asked.

My brow dipped. I couldn't read his tone or his expression.

"You just looked like you were into whatever you were doing and I didn't want to distract you," I spoke up trailing him down the ladder. An involuntary grunt left my lips while he flexed his muscles.

"Don't look at me like a piece of meat," he shot back before letting a smile grace his lips.

I flashed red and chuckled through my embarrassment. "You flexed. Willie what am I supposed to do? Do you want to get lunch or am I going to have to go alone and be hit on by some random man?"

The way the jealousy flashed over his face, with his mouth balled up, my embarrassment fell flat. I couldn't understand how we were grown and standing here like to lovestruck puppies.

"What's on the menu?" he finally asked, looking me up and down.

I turned on my heels and started to open the door. "I thought you would see it my way."

"It ain't got nothing to do with seeing it your way. It has everything to do with you carrying your fine ass across the street trying to get a nigga's head knocked off his shoulders," he gruffly spoke up walking out the door behind me. "Too damn fine to be playing with me like that."

NINE

W illie

"YOU REALLY NEED to stop looking at me like that," she spoke up from behind her menu.

"You can't even see me, Ladybug," I commented back refusing to take my eyes off of her.

"I can feel it," she muttered. "And it's fuckin' heavy."

Aria dropped her menu and shoved her hand through her hair. "Why are you doing this?"

"Don't act like you ain't enjoying it," I said with a chuckle.

I didn't know how much longer I could go without putting my hands on her and burying myself deep inside of her walls. She was flustered from me looking at her. If she knew the thoughts that kept me up at night and kept the cold water running for hours we would not be here. All the glances and cute shit was nice, but I was a grown man. I was pacing this shit out of complete respect for her. Had it been up to me, Ladybug would have been mine the second I laid my eyes on her.

I was irritated with all of this shit. She really had the nerve to strut her ass past me looking good and smelling better. Not to mention she walked in late as hell and didn't speak. I prided myself on being laid back but Aria was testing me. I should have snatched her ass up and ended this shit. But the build up would have her pretty ass making my house a home and building a family with me.

Her light giggle snapped me out of my head. "Whether or not I'm enjoying it doesn't matter."

"Bullshit, Ladybug. I can tell how you squirming in your seat that you're playing around with them nasty ass thoughts in your head."

She gasped and looked around the cafe. "William James! Shut up!"

Sitting back in my seat I laughed at her reaction. I ran my hand over my beard, "Don't even act up in these people's establishment, woman. I've met your momma."

Aria flailed her arms and rolled her eyes. "My momma is a damn mess, and she knows it."

"And the apple don't fall far from the tree."

She bit her lip again.

"I will give you every reason in your head to bite that lip, Ladybug."

"Willie James Bernett. You finally stopped ducking and dodging and came to see me," Chanel came bouncing around the corner with her tattooed breasts on full display. She stopped at the table and leaned in closer to me prompting me to lean back.

"I'm actually here with, Ladybug," I quickly corrected, throwing my head over to Aria.

Chanel's presence halted our conversation, and removed the smile from my baby's face. I didn't like that at all. Chanel needed to get her ass on before she ruined our moment or worse.

"Oh," she replied with a faint frown. "Hi Aria. How's everything with your divorce?"

Aria squinted and leaned up on her elbows. Chanel was playing with fire and I wasn't trying to tell her that the iron was hot. She was going to have to figure that out on her own.

"I'm sorry what does that have to do with the reason you're standing here. Is it to brick with Willie, or take our orders because he hasn't eaten all day and neither have I…"

Chanel drew her neck back before slowly removing her breasts out my face and pulling out her notepad. "You didn't have to be so nasty about it."

Aria snorted in laughter. "The only one being nasty is you. You've been throwing yourself at him for how long and nothing? I'm getting the cobb salad with the house ranch, Willie what are you eating?"

Shit, you later.

"A turkey club double meat and waffle fries."

Aria's tone switched up so quickly with Chanel, even I knew not to look at her as I handed over the menu. When Chanel dragged herself away from the table, I watched Aria attempt to rid herself of the aggravation the Chanel caused.

"Jealousy is cute on you," I commented, making her dart me a warning glare.

"No one is jealous, Willie."

"That's what you're telling yourself, hm?"

A slight roll of the eyes and a huff. "Why would I be jealous of that? If that's what you want, that's fine."

"You are the most hard headed woman on the face of this earth, and you drive me crazy. You ain't been listening to shit I've been saying to you, have you?"

"I heard you, Willie."

"So why you acting like I won't snatch your ass up and end all these games we're playin?" I fired back watching her shift in her seat again. "Talking that shit gon get your check cashed."

"You are not obligated to me."

I licked my lips and leaned in so I could grab her full atten-tion. "You're trying to take a nigga being laid back as a reason to fight this shit when I'm really trying to make you an edible arrangement, and give you my last name."

She gulped.

"What if I was, Ladybug? I see your wheels turning, and I know damn well why you keep shifting like that."

She opened her mouth and no sound came out.

"You don't have to say nothing," I replied with a chuckle. "I made a promise to you though. Ain't touching your temple until it's time."

"Then what are we doing?" She was gnawing away at her lip.

"We're going to eat lunch, talk some shit through, and then I'm taking you to dinner."

Aria seemed to relax her ways when I stepped in and set her back on track. The more I laid back and let her have her way the more she tried to run away from what she knew. She belonged here with me; anchored at my side, fused into my rib.

After we left Jenine's, we checked on the shop before driving out to the lake. No distractions, just her and I staring up at the changing sky. Without a doubt, I wanted her blessing me with her covering, but I knew she needed more than that. I was going to give her more than she dreamed she deserved.

"Why are you so fascinated by me, Willie? Other men look at me and see a divorced woman with baggage but you look at me like it's the first time all over again," she asked with her head resting on my chest.

My hand was molded into the dip of her hip, and my nose inhaled the hibiscus and coconut oil in her hair. "Because I knew you before that, and it's my mission to take all the baggage, unpack it, organize it, and throw out what you don't have space for. I'm going to love you so damn good you're not going to have room or time to think about what happened before me."

Her breathing hitched as she sat up and peered down at me. Her deep ember eyes danced with a flame I never saw before.

She'd thrown her inhibitions to the wind, stopped toying with the what if's, and acted on what we both were feeling since I followed her into the shop a couple weeks ago.

Aria's cashmere hands cupped my face and mine did the same. My thumbs brushed over her lips before I attacked them. She kissed me back feverishly while our tongues wrestled, hands clung to each other's clothing. Gripping her throat gently, I nibbled at her plush lips and pulled away.

"Nah, you ain't ready for me yet, baby."

It took her a minute to pull herself together. She nodded. "Can we talk and walk?"

Obliging her request, I held her close while the moonlight guided us around the lake's beaten path and back to the car. The fifteen year old boy in me was giddy and shit, while the grown man was relishing in the moment. Aria was sitting in my pick up truck with her hand wrapped around mine. Everything was coming full circle, I could only pray she didn't get cold feet and run off.

TEN

ria

THE LAST COUPLE of days with Willie had renewed my hope in falling in love again. Everything I wanted in my marriage, I had now. I was smiling uncontrollably, listening, and laying my stubbornness down. Well, I thought about it. I wouldn't be me if I didn't push back. More than anything, he made me comfortable enough to be me.

Willie had never disrespected me or anyone else - even Chanel. I found his temperament to be the sexiest thing. My body reacted to him naturally; how damn good he looked.

I didn't know how long I'd been standing at the kitchen sink drying this one glass. I didn't even realize that I'd been drooling at the sight of him in cutting momma's grass. Every muscle on his golden back glistened under the light layer of sweat. His butt was tight along with his calves. Nothing compared to watching him push the mower toward the house in those gray jogger shorts.

As bad as I wanted him to just take me, I could see why he was easing me into that realm with him. Willie was blessed in every department, and the print outlined against his leg told me all I needed to know. After one hit of that I would be walking different, talking different, and finding reasons to fight just to make up. My panties were ruined at this point, and I didn't know how I was going to get through dinner without wanting dessert first.

Everything I heard in church was now out the window. I was finding things around momma's house to fix, move, or dust so I could keep my eyes on him. Silently thanking God he didn't get up in time for church this morning because these impure thoughts were not allowed in the house of God.

"Aria," my mother's voice flowed out the kitchen causing me to damn near jump out of my skin.

Turning around on the heels of my feet I was met by her knowing look, and a tray of her famous lemonade. "Thirsty?"

I cleared my throat and brushed my pressed hair out of my face. "I'm fine, momma."

"That you may be, but you're just as thirsty as you are fine. I have watched you watch that man like a hawk for the last hour. You've washed clean dishes out the dishwasher, you've gawked in awe, and you almost drooled in my pot of greens. Take this and give the man something to drink."

"Momma," I started up as I took the tray out of her hand.

"Go give the man something to drink," she directed, opening the front door and waving me out of her presence. "With a smile on that beautiful face."

I cut her a look as I walked out of the house and shuffled onto the porch in my yellow flowy dress that was now clinging to my curves thanks to the wind. Willie was walking back from the shed and wiping his face with his shirt.

"Are you thirsty?" I asked a few seconds after I came into his view.

He paused for a moment, undressed me with his eyes and lightly grunted before coming closer to the porch. I tried my damndest to look into his beautiful orbs, but the python inching down his thigh was making it hard for me to focus.

"I could use a drink," he spoke up, climbing the steps and towering over me. Once again, his eyes roamed over me before he hooked my chin and kissed my lips gently. "You look damn good, Ladybug."

"Why thank you."

Turning around to walk away from him I heard him hum, "mm mm mm."

Sitting the tray down, I leaned over enough to give him something else to gawk over as I poured him a glass. Willie teasingly brushed past me. "Don't play with me at your momma's house. You know she's somewhere watching, and I ain't trying to give her a show."

I clamped down on my lip feeling him grip my hip before sitting down. Tossing my hair over my shoulder I handed him a glass before I sat down across from him and looked over the yard. "Thank you for doing this for her."

"Don't mention it," he spoke up. I didn't have to look at him to feel his eyes peeling my dress off of me. "You wore that to church?"

I nodded.

"I might be up on time next week."

I licked my lips and tried to shake my head clear. "What else is on your to do list?"

"Besides you?" he asked, making my head whip around. "Repaint the railing."

I slowly stood up and cleared my throat. "I'll leave you to it."

"Come back and check on me, Ladybug. I might need some sugar to keep me going."

I blew him a kiss and walked back in the house. I needed a cold shower immediately. Staying clear of the windows, I finished helping momma with dinner and tried to occupy myself with a slew of other things than thinking about how much vitamin D I needed.

"Willie, did you get everything?" I heard mom ask as she brought the tray of lemonade back inside the house.

I leaned on the wall and watched Willie watch me. "Yes, ma'am. I would stay for dinner but I didn't bring anything decent to join you beautiful ladies."

"I understand," momma replied. "You know where to find me when you need a good home cooked meal."

"I sure do." He flashed her a polite smile and looked back at me. "Ladybug, I'll be seeing you."

"See you," I softly replied.

He nodded and excused himself out the door frame. Momma closed it and looked at me. "Come here girl."

Trekking behind her into the kitchen to see her place the lemonade on the counter and pour it into a separate container. In order not to run out the house behind Willie, I grabbed a plate and helped myself to dinner.

"Put it down girl," she spoke up again.

"But momma I'm hungry," I whined as she took the plate out my hands.

"I'll say," she huffed. She put my plate back in the cabinet and started fixing tupperware containers of food. "You are going to take this over to him. Give him an hour though to shower, get a beer and unwind. You're going to stop by your place, freshen and blot your face."

"Momma, this isn't the first time I've rode a bike."

She stopped and grinned at me. "Oh, but baby girl that ain't a bike. I am praying that this is the last."

"I feel like you're trying to pimp me out," I groaned, as if I didn't need William James turning me inside out and ending all this teasing he'd been doing to me.

"I feel like you need that press sweated out, and your ass spanked. But what do I know?" she asked with a shrug.

"Momma!"

"Oh, baby. Drop the act, take that man this food and feed him, if you know what I mean," she finalized packing everything up and handing the bag over to me. "We'll talk soon."

"Uh huh, we sure will."

ELEVEN

illie

"YOU KNOW ARIA IS BACK."

Sharing the news with my mother, I shuffled to the fridge to grab a beer. After the week I had, I needed the whole damn case and some good ass sleep. Soon as I finished this call with my mother, it was on my radar. Sleep would keep me from driving over to her place and violating her sexy ass. As much as I wasn't trying to pull myself from Mrs. McFee's house or her daughter, I needed to. Every urge I'd been trying to suppress all week was telling on me. By the way Ladybug was leering over me, it was evident trouble and good loving were on the horizon.

"Well, I hope this time you actually keep her put," she shared in her warm drawl. "You know you let her slip right on out of your fingers that last time."

I huffed and popped the top off of my bottle. Taking a swig, I leaned on the counter. "You don't need to remind me. I know what I did."

"Good, now what are you doing to fix it?" she quizzed.

My mom was team Aria through and through. Of course she would never tell Aria that, she liked to see people sweat and put their best foot forward when they were dealing with her. And Aria always came with bottomless charm, sarcasm, and spunk so she passed with flying colors in that department early.

"I'm getting there."

"Getting there ain't fixing it, Willie. You need to make sure you get your woman," she coached. "I raised you to be a gentleman, not a pussy. Snatch her ass up and tell her what it's going to be. Be prepared to get hit because she likes to fight, but stand firm."

I couldn't help but laugh. "I hear you, ma."

"Uh huh," she snorted. "You can hear me all you want. I believe I told you this before she went away and married that boy."

The doorbell rang saving me from having to comment. Assuming it was one of the neighbors I didn't think twice before opening the door. Ladybug was standing on the other side holding an insulated bag of food. She smiled up at me and said, "you didn't eat."

Licking my lips, I stepped back and let her prance her fine ass in my house and walk straight to the kitchen. Judging by the way her ass bounced back and forth under the dress, she didn't have on any panties.

"Willie, did you hear me?" mom forcibly asked as I grunted.

"Yeah, but I'm going to have to call you back, ma. She just walked in."

"Oh shit, snatch her up!" She was so loud I knew Aria heard from her where she stood unpacking the food. "Love you, bye."

I pulled the phone away from my ear after hearing it end and strolled into the kitchen. Positioning myself behind her, I wrapped my hands around her waist so she could feel what her presence and scent had done to me. I was fully awake and dessert was on the menu.

"How do you want me to fix your plate?" her voice was smooth. It was an attempt to keep her cool while my hand roamed over the fabric of her dress and my lips caressed her exposed skin. "I brought over some lemonade too."

"Only thing I want on my plate is you. All this other shit can wait until later." I tugged at the sleeve of her dress so I could nibble on her flesh.

A light moan escaped her lips. "I came over here to feed you, Willie."

"Then let me eat," I growled.

In one swift move I had her spun around, staring at me with low eyes, waiting for my next move. A sinister flash of energy glimmered in her eyes before she ran her hands down my bare chest to the top of my basketball shorts. She attacked my lips while sliding her tiny hands into my shorts and wrapping her hand around the base of my dick.

Aria's soft lips left mine and traveled down my body, allowing her free hand to tug my shorts down. My eyes dropped as she lowered herself into a squat with her heels still on, giving her the lift she needed to be eye level with my dick.

She didn't attack it immediately. She took her time and admired it. "Willie, you should have snatched me up weeks ago."

I tried replying but the heat and wetness of her mouth met the hardness of my dick in the process of her pushing her lips down on my shit. I hissed, my toes curled, and my hands planted themselves in her hair. Ladybug swirled her tongue around while bobbing up and down. Every so often she would kiss the head, nibble at it, and go back to work. The mixture of pleasure and pain was driving me over the edge.

Aria's hands went from my thighs to the base and began twisting while she sucked, slurped, and moaned.

"Ladybug," I groaned, throwing my head back. Firmly holding her still, I stroked in and out of her cheeks. "Where do you want it?"

She flashed those ember eyes up and groaned with me still inside her cheeks, "Right here."

She went back to work until my seeds were going down the back of her throat. Like a champ, she swallowed and slurped me dry. This was going to be the last time she had me whimpering like this tonight.

When she released me I pulled her up, tore her dress from her frame and sat her on the counter. Roughly parting her thighs,

I admired her pretty pussy glistening under the recessed lighting of the kitchen.

Wasting no more time, I pushed her legs up and buried my face in her essence. She tasted better than I imagined. The way she sang my name was going to have her folded up, bent over and receiving me the rest of the night. But first, I was going to write my name all over her with my tongue.

"Ah, shiiiiiii," she slurred holding on to the edge of the counter. "Please don't stop, Willie."

She was dripping down my beard and over my counter. Pushing a finger inside of her opening made her gasp. It was a damn shame her body had been neglected like this. Granted, I had full advantage to show her how she should have been loved.

"You taste so good, baby," I groaned inside of her folds as her body started to shake. "That's the last one you get without permission."

TWELVE

ria

HOW THE HELL did I ignore this man for so long? Willie was certainly a gentleman in the streets but what he did to my body was the work of a rough necked nigga that sold drugs for a living. I couldn't get enough. I didn't want to get enough. My sona wave had nothing on how he stretched me and made my body clamp down on him.

He was well endowed, and I knew my uterus may have been knocked out the frame. That was a risk I was willing to take. Willie was not going to be able to get rid of me after this. He was mine, and anyone sniffing around him would have to see me about it.

He glided his body over mine with ease. My legs were all over the place. One was wrapped in his custody and the other was pushed over my head.

"You were made for me, baby," he growled.

Every look and praise he gave me only made me flood more. I never had this reaction to any man. From last night into this morning, Willie had me creaming, following directions, and refusing to sleep for long.

He leaned down to push himself inside me deeper to kiss my lips. "You can't leave me again."

I felt his warmth coat my walls. It was a feeling I was getting accustomed to. It was Willie. If anything were to form from all of this lovemaking, I was confident we would be elated. Not to mention our mothers would leap for joy.

Willie placed one final kiss to my lips before dropping to his back. "Good morning, gorgeous."

I let my legs fall and my heart rate calm down before I rolled to my side and kissed his chest. "Good morning. How'd you sleep?"

"Best sleep of my life."

"Considering we only slept for a few hours," I said with a sigh. "I have to go to the shop."

"No you don't," he spoke while finding the strength to push himself out of the bed and walk to the bathroom. "Baby after all of that I know you can't walk. I'll call Ares, have him handle whatever you need, and we'll go check on everything tomorrow."

Ares was Willie's right hand man, and because he trusted him with the day to day things of his business, I did too. I didn't even conjure up the energy to combat him on it.

"Willie, I will be able to walk," I sassed throwing my sore legs over the bed. The second I stood up and my thighs met, I felt the aftermath of receiving the best sex of my life. Wincing softly, I tried to slowly walk into the bathroom behind him.

"You feel that shit don't you," he asked with a chuckle. "Big daddy tore that thang up."

Willie was sitting on the edge of the tub watching the water flow from the faucet. I stopped in front of him and glanced at us in the mirror. His hands found my hips and his mouth gently kissed my stomach.

"We look good together," I commented with a smile.

"I've been trying to tell you that for damn near twenty years. I'll tell you for another twenty if I have to, Ladybug."

The look on his face was different. It was soft and accomplished. "I wouldn't mind that, but I'm not running."

"I know, I made sure of that. Even if you try you won't get far," he replied with another chuckle. "Get in and relax. I'm going to call Ares."

After ensuring I safely climbed inside of the hot water, Willie and all his gifts strolled out of the bathroom.

I must have fallen asleep. When I opened my eyes the water was cold and I could hear pots and pans banging in the kitchen. I washed off in the cold water and got myself out to go see what Willie was doing. From experience, I knew he could cook but everything sounded like a disaster. I used his lotion to rub into my skin and then found one of his shirts in the second drawer I opened.

Turning the corner to the kitchen, I couldn't help but laugh at him covered in pancake mix. "That is not how Aunt Jemima wanted you to cook that."

"Aunt Jemima ain't got a dime in this company." He shot me a defeated look while he tried wiping his face off. "You ain't supposed to be seeing this struggle."

I rounded the counter and dusted the flour from his tattooed chest with minimal hair at the center. "Well, baby. It's all or nothing now. How about I do breakfast today at my place?"

He smiled faintly and looked at his mess. "That might be a good idea. Plus, I can finally see if you can cook or not."

"Boy don't insult me," I teased before I leaned over to get the spare towel.

"Keep flashing me that pussy and I'll assault you."

"Oh big daddy, it ain't assault if I'm asking for it."

He bit his lip and grunted as he pulled me into his hard body. "As much as I want to dive back into your ocean and drink your nectar. Your body needs a break."

He kissed my neck followed by a slap on the ass. "Let's get this shit cleaned up so I can take you home and put some panties on you before I backtrack."

After he turned around to finish cleaning up his mess, I watched him for a moment. Taking all of this in my heart skipped beats; my stomach twisted and turned with butterflies and revelations. "I can't believe I walked away from you."

Willie finished what he was doing then turned to look at me. "You walked away because I let you. That was the worst mistake of my life, and I regretted every moment of it."

"I hate to admit this," I started with a sigh and a swat to my matted hair. "I did too."

I dropped my eyes and fought the emotion building. "I knew where my heart was, and I tried so hard to fight that shit and deny that I made a mistake. I guess had I stayed, I wouldn't be able to appreciate who you are."

Willie closed the gap between us and cupped my chin. "As much as I hated that it took us so long, it needed to happen. I had to go through some shit to be your man. But Ladybug, I ain't going nowhere, and neither are you. I'll tie your pretty ass up if I have to."

I grinned. "You don't have to tie me up to get me to stay, just tie me up and make me cum."

He kissed me passionately and broke away right before he got worked up again. "I got some shorts in the bottom drawer, go put them on before we don't make it out of here. I also owe you a new dress."

"You sure do," I threw over my shoulder as I walked away.

When we got to my condo, Willie made himself busy with taking the trash out while I hopped in the shower to condition my hair. Once my hair was detangled and my curls were popping, I scurried into the kitchen to make his breakfast. The need to take care of him was increasing by the second. I suppose good sex and finally accepting the fact that Willie was my person and I was his, activated something different in me.

"Ares is going to take care of the shop today. He said he got your shipment," Willie spoke up as he twisted another light bulb over the door. "And he'll put everything away for you."

I'd been meaning to change it but every time I thought about it I got irritated with the process. I was short and I wore heels constantly to keep me at the average height. Changing the bulb would mean that I would have to stand on a chair and strain.

"Thank you," I said, flashing him a smile over my shoulder while I whipped the eggs. "I'm almost done if you want to go wash your hands and sit down."

"You don't have to thank me, Ladybug."

The rest of the day was surrounded around cat naps, movies, stolen kisses and another round of good loving in the shower. The man made me feel like an arrangement made for eating, remnants of our love was still on my skin. Every inch of me glowed. My heart was settled, and I never wanted to leave this space with him.

He was mine, and I was his. There was no turning back.

THIRTEEN

W illie

TWO MONTHS HAD GONE BY, and it felt like I blinked. Time with Aria flashed before my eyes. Every moment I had with her was a blessing, losing West taught me that. Weston also told me to lock her down when she came back. It took a month to convince her that I couldn't sleep without her, and another to get her out of her lease to move in with me.

The house was livelier, there was a pep in my step, and pretending like I was happy faded into the background. Aria was the light of my world, and whatever I needed to do to keep her with me I was going to do it.

"Are you going to tell me where we are going?" she asked, walking out the bed room in a magenta dress that fell over her curves effortlessly. Her face was made up and her curly hair fell around her face.

She stopped short of me to wrestle with the earring she was trying to get in her ear. Glancing over me at me she did it again. "William James Bernett are you wearing a suit?"

"I am," I smoothly answered.

"Hmm," she buzzed, looking me over as she grabbed her clutch off of the counter top. "Tonight must be special if you're wearing a suit."

"Every night with you is special, Ladybug."

She smirked arrogantly and strutted past me. "I know, it is. Are you ready?"

"I've been waiting on you for an hour," I shot back, grabbing her keys off of the counter.

"Was it worth it?" she asked as she walked out the door.

I took in the sight of her ass bouncing back and forth like a volleyball. These days her ass was wider and poking out. My handiwork was on full display. Ladybug was getting thick. "Sure as hell was. You're looking good enough to eat."

"Because I am good enough to eat," she sassed carefully, stepping down the stairs while I secured the house.

Meeting her where she was, I took her hand and led her down the rest of the way to the car. "Edible arrangement."

She giggled girlishly and climbed into the car after I palmed her ass.

I rode into town with her hand wrapped around mine. "We got to make a stop by the shop before dinner."

"Oh good, I wanted to see those fixtures you put up," she replied looking out the window. "I'm so nervous about next week. It's making me sick."

"You got it baby. Ain't nothing you touch that doesn't turn into gold. Myself included."

Proverbs 18:22 had shown up and showed out in my life. Since Aria and I made this official, I'd gotten contracts from here to Ganton Hills to restore buildings and redesign houses. It was so much work that I put Ares over some of the big projects I had in town. He was deserving of a shot and reminded me a lot of myself. Any chance that I had to help out I was going to.

"I could say the same," she replied with a hum.

It got quiet until we pulled up at the shop and her mouth fell open and her eyes grew big. The shop was lit up and completely set for the grand opening next week. Before it got crazy, I wanted her to stand in the middle of her dream surrounded by the people who loved her and were proud of her.

"William," she crooned cutting me a look. "What are you doing?"

I killed the engine and got out of the car. After rounding the back, I opened her door and helped her out. "Celebrating you because you deserve it."

"I don't know how you got this past me, and I don't know how anybody in this town kept it to themselves either."

My hand rested on the small of her back as she walked up to her shop and stopped to look at the large wooden sign hanging over the building. Mocha and Merlot was scripted in purple letters. As she stepped inside the building she was greeted by my mother, her mother, and a handful of people from church. Yeah, she had me up and there every Sunday.

"Aria!" my mother excitedly screeched pulling her into a tight embrace. "Love looks good on you, you're getting thick."

"That's all me, mom. Give my credit."

Aria slapped my chest, coupling it with a look. "Reverend Harris is here."

"Ladybug, they know. Your ass is poking out."

She rolled her eyes and strutted away from me to greet the rest of the guests. I loved how she could work a room and make everyone feel welcomed and loved. I sat back until the time was right to get everyone's attention and do what I really came here to do.

Gently hitting the glass prompting everyone to look my way. "I want to thank you all for coming out tonight, and keeping this a secret from Ladybug because she's nosey and has asked me three times where we were going tonight and why."

The crowd laughed lightly and nodded in agreement.

"This year has been by far the toughest but for me it's been the most rewarding. We all lost Weston, but he left us a lot behind to keep pushing forward. One thing he left me with was strict instructions. One with business and two was Ladybug. Baby can you come here."

"Williiiieeeee." She sang my name as only she could as she sauntered over to me. "What are you up to?"

I kissed her cheek and winked. "You'll see."

"Oh, boy."

Aria darted her eyes around the crowd before I pulled her attention back to me. "Ladybug, you know I always loved you. You know that my heart was always meant for you and you were always made to be my rib."

Aria tucked her lip between her teeth and nodded. "I do."

"West knew it too. He kind of held my feet to the fire in preparation for your return. I've been holding on to this engagement ring for a year and two months," I announced. I could hear the crowd behind us growing anxious. My attention was Aria's. Her lip trembled and her hands shook.

I pulled the ring box from my pocket and lowered myself down to one knee. Taking her hand in mine, I kissed her knuckles and continued with my speech. "I promised Weston I was going to make an honorable woman out of you. I told him if I ever had another chance to show you good love, I would. I told him that our children will know that he was that man. But more than anything, I promised him that I would love you until the world stopped. I love all that you are, Aria McFee. You are my church, my Sunday morning, and my edible arrangement. Beautiful to my eyes, joy to my soul, and sweet on my lips. Baby, will you marry me?"

Aria licked her dry lips and placed her hands on my shoulders. Leaning in to me she whispered in my ear, "Will you be my baby daddy?"

She was trying to make me break down in front of all of these people. "You're for real, Ladybug?"

"I am," she spoke just above a whisper. "We are. I don't want anything else than what God has for us. Yes, I will marry you a million times over."

Adorning her hand with the ring, I kissed her knuckles again then her stomach. I stood to my feet, grabbed her chin, and kissed the hell out of her. Cheers and claps hit our eardrums and I felt our mothers wrap their arms around us.

"Y'all know you're having this wedding before she starts showing," my mom spoke up. "I've been waiting for him to do this for eight years. Eight."

Aria's smile was unmatched. She kissed me one last time before she was pulled away to talk to everyone who came through to celebrate us.

"You and Weston always had something up your sleeves," Mrs. McFee started up with an elbow nudge to my side. "He's so happy, I can feel it. Before he left, he was so concerned about who was going to take care of her. We've all wanted this since we saw that spark ignite between you two. Take care of my baby, she's all I have left, Willie."

Naturally, I wrapped my arms around Mrs. McFee and kissed her cheek. "You have both of us now."

FOURTEEN

A^{ria}

MY NERVES WERE in my ass. It was like I'd never been married before but this was forever. It was Willie and I against the world, now.

I stood in my old room running my hand over this silk cream dress. My belly was still small at five months. I was thankful for it, however, the day where our little bean would pop out and slow me down was coming.

Before I completely lost my shit, I sucked in a deep breath and closed my eyes. "I know you're here. I can feel you. I just needed to say thank you for leading me home. I'm going to be okay, Weston. You and daddy get me down this aisle and then you can rest. I promise."

A faint knock on the door prompted me to wipe my face and grab my bouquet full of pink and orange roses. Mom popped her head in and gleamed at the sight of me. "You're radiant."

"I heard a baby will do that to you."

"That and good loving. I am so proud of you, and so happy for you. You finally got your happily ever after. Another adventure for you. Remember that it's you two. Nothing else matters. Don't stop loving hard, and never lose that fire that keeps you going back for more. Tomorrow isn't promised, tell him how you feel and do the same for him. This is the last ride."

The bubbling joy took over my face. This was the first day of the rest of my life, and I was anxious to get it started. I reached for momma's hand, squeezing it when she laced her fingers in mine.

From the living room, Why I Love You by MAJOR graced my ears. The joy was causing tears to spring into my eyes. The double doors opened, through the drapery, the flowers, and the fifty people who came to celebrate with us, all I could see was Willie's beautiful face twitch while he attempted to hold the tears back.

I took one step out to the porch, and he took off toward me. Reverend Harris had to stop him from running down the aisle toward me. A soft chortle left my lips while I marched toward him, hand in hand with momma.

Willie wiped his eyes again and mouthed, "you're beautiful."

I blushed as if it were the first time. This was a feeling I never wanted to die. I was marching toward the love of my life carrying the child we created in the height of passion. My life was complete. Nothing else would do but this. Willie had a way that he loved me, that was unrivaled.

Momma and I stopped at the foot of the altar, and my eyes didn't leave the orbs of my love. He looked as handsome as ever in his vest, oxford button down and black tuxedo pants. It was late fall in the south and it was still hot, I wasn't even going to fight him on the tux jacket.

After my mother relinquished me into his care, they hugged, and she took her seat. Everything else was white noise compared to the I love you's Willie was mouthing, paired with you are so beautiful and I can't wait to get you home.

"The couple has chosen to write their own vows," Reverend Harris spoke up.

I took a deep breath and swiped Willie's tears away. "You have been my constant. My light in the darkest time. The safest place I've known for twenty years. You've been mine before I knew you were. I vow to love you, respect you, always be there when you need me, and remain at your side no matter what life throws at us. I love you from the depths of my soul, William, and I will never stop."

"Ladybug, loving you has forced me to love me better. You're the reason I wake up, the reason I go to sleep, the reason I further myself everyday. We are our wildest dreams. I vow to honor your mind, your heart, and your spirit. Respect your ideas, cultivate them, and plant seeds in our garden that will grow into generations of kings and queens who will know the power of love and patience. I love you Aria. You are mine, and I am forever yours."

Before the rings were exchanged, I looked out to the crowd and saw the photo of our dad's and Weston, smiling, in their respective seats. The people who loved us, our mother's who linked arms, and we were engulfed in the breeze. There was nothing else I needed. I had it all. Turns out all I needed to be happy was to return to where it all started.

"Ladies and gentlemen, I present to you, Mr. and Mrs. William James Bernett. Willie, I know you've been waiting for a long time for this, kiss your bride."

We clashed into each other as our lips molded into one another's and our tongues wrestled.

"Mrs. Bernett, you're mine now."

"I was always yours, Mr. Bernett."

"Damn right."

THE END

ACKNOWLEDGMENTS

Thank you for reading Edible Arrangements. Willie and Aria were so fun to write.

If you are looking for something else to read, see my catalog below. Until next time, TMC.

See you between the pages.

ABOUT THE AUTHOR

Cassandra B is a sub brand under Aubree Pynn.

APXCB provides love stories with bold men and women receiving the love they demand on their terms.

CPSIA information can be obtained
at www.ICGtesting.com
Printed in the USA
LVHW081623061120
670969LV00011B/1263